TWISTED TALES

The Dripping Head
&
Other Gruesome Stories

By R. C. Welch

Illustrated by Scott Fike

CHECKERBOARD PRESS

NEW YORK

*For my grandmother, who spoiled me rotten
and still does whenever I give her the chance.*
—R.C.W.

*To my parents who had to raise me,
their own little monster.*
—S. F.

Published by Checkerboard Press, Inc.
30 Vesey Street, New York, NY 10007

Table of Contents

The Dripping Head 5

The Stranger 15

School Games 27

On the Radio 39

Talk to the Animals 49

Mirror Image 63

Crack Up There 75

A Jarring Experience 87

The Write Stuff 97

A Family Outing 109

Photo Finish 119

The Dripping Head

R yan was poking around in the storeroom of his parents' antique store. He liked coming back here and digging through the huge collection of junk that his mom and dad gathered from around the world in their efforts to find really valuable stuff.

They had just gotten a whole truckload of books from Malaysia. He had heard his parents telling one of their friends that some guy had died and his family was selling everything he had owned.

Ryan was going through one of the boxes, which was filled with books, bundles of letters, and some old photos. He was taking out and examining everything before setting it down wherever there was space. Near the bottom of the box he came across a small book with a lock across the pages. "Hmm," he said under his breath, "this looks interesting."

He pulled his prize out and blew a cloud of dust off it. It seemed very old, with dust rubbed into the cracked leather. He pulled at the clasp, but it wouldn't open. He pried the corners as far apart as he could to peek at the pages inside.

"What are you doing?" Ryan's mother asked as she came into the storeroom.

Ryan closed the book guiltily. "Just looking, Mom. Why?"

His mother smiled and put her hands on her hips. "If you're going to pull everything out of the boxes, the least you could do is stack them in some kind of order!"

Ryan glanced around at the books he had scattered around the room. "Um, sorry."

His mother chuckled and leaned over him. "All right. What have you found?"

He held up his discovery for his mother to examine.

"Looks like a diary," she said. She also tried to open the clasp. "Huh. Was there a key anywhere in that box?"

"Nope."

"Well, there's only one solution, then." She pulled a carton cutter out of her jeans and sliced through the thin leather strap that sealed the pages. Then she opened the book and leafed through the old diary. After a quick look, she handed it back to Ryan.

"Let me know if it says anything interesting," she said. "I've got to get the rest of this stuff sorted out."

She grabbed a box that Ryan hadn't gotten to yet. "Oh. Will you please make sure it all ends up back in the same box it came from?"

Ryan nodded and turned his attention to the volume in his hands. He opened it slowly, feeling the paper crinkle in his hands.

The pages were yellow with age and the ink, faded. He read aloud the inscription on the inside of the front cover, "For Mona." The writing was in big, curvy letters that were difficult to make out, but at least it was in English. Ryan thumbed idly through the book, stopping to read passages that looked interesting.

About halfway through the diary, he found a small black-and-white photo of a young woman. He continued reading, and soon found out that she was the daughter of the man whose diary he held. She had died giving birth to a son. The grandfather spent a few pages describing how sad he was. Ryan began skimming again, until a strange word caught his eye.

It awoke.

It hadn't been truly asleep. But what was left of its mind couldn't think of a better word. It opened its eyes and rolled them in their sockets. Everything was black. It tried to move but couldn't feel anything below its neck. It lay still, hating whatever it was that had called it back to this horrible existence.

It felt something.

At first, it couldn't remember the word. Then it did—*hunger*. It was hungry, so hungry it was agony to lie still. It tried again to move, but couldn't. It screamed in a high, breathless voice. The hunger was driving it mad. It had to eat! It began whipping its head from side to side, and realized it was in a narrow space. It brought its head up, and felt wood against its forehead.

Hunger and hatred defined its existence. It had to do something. To go somewhere. Then it could eat. But where? Something would tell it. Somehow it would know. It had to be ready.

Gathering all its effort, it rammed its head forward. The old wood splintered, and it saw pale light. It slammed its head again, and the wood fell away.

It was in a small stone room. A low moon outlined the empty interior through a high window. It saw carved angels perched in the corners of the room, but did not understand their significance. Thoughts and images flickered in its ruined brain like far-off flashes of lightning, but it did not bother to interpret them. It felt something tear at its neck as it lifted itself up and searched for an exit.

———

The natives call it Penanngga Lan, Ryan read in the old man's diary. *I don't know whether to laugh or berate them for such nonsense. I think I shall have to devise a means to prove to them that their fears are baseless.*

Ryan sat back. "Great," he said out loud. "But what is he talking about?"

"What's that, dear?" his mother asked as she came in to grab another box.

Ryan gestured to the diary. "It's some old guy's diary. He writes kind of funny, but I can understand it."

"Anything interesting?" She paused in the doorway, setting her box on a shelf.

Ryan shrugged. "Not really. Hey, Mom, do you know what a Penanngga Lan is?"

"No, what?"

"I don't know! This guy's talking about one. I think it's some kind of Malaysian word."

"Well, why don't you look in some of those old dictionaries?" she said, pointing to a box behind Ryan. She picked up another carton. "After I log this bunch I've got to run down to Jasmin's for a little while. Will you be okay alone?"

Ryan nodded. "Sure."

"All right, honey. I should be back in about an hour."

Ryan nodded again and started pawing through the box behind him for a dictionary.

<hr/>

It was outside. It didn't notice the warm air or the soft breeze. All it could think about was the call. The call that would guide it. The call that had brought the gnawing hunger. To answer the call would end its misery.

<hr/>

"Ah hah!" exclaimed Ryan. He sat down with his back propped against a battered desk and read the brief entry in the *Dictionary of Malayan Myth and Legend*.

"This foul creature is always female, and often

a woman who has died in childbirth. At night, the head of a Penanngga Lan will detach itself from its body and fly through the air trailing its internal organs behind it. A Penanngga Lan subsists by drinking human blood, preferably that of small children. It is said that the mere sight of this monster flying through the air will drive a person insane."

Ryan closed the book and leaned his head back, amazed.

"Wow," he breathed. Then he grabbed for the diary. He found where he had left off, and began reading it more closely. The old man described how he came to believe that his daughter had become a Penanngga Lan. And of the battle he and the village shaman fought to imprison the creature in its tomb.

Even now I find it hard to believe it is over. Over?! I scarcely believe it ever happened! But her name is chiseled off the tombstone, and erased from the family records. I shall write it once only, before I close this diary for the last time, and the knowledge of this will go with me to my grave. As the name rests, so shall she.

Ryan stared at the last entry.
Then he slowly turned back to the opening inscription. "Mona, huh?" he muttered. "Pretty weird."

The call came again. It traveled with the darkness, sliding along the shadowy edge of the advancing night. Soon it would feed.

———

After a little while, Ryan shook himself and got up. He looked at the photograph again.

"Okay," he said out loud, just to break the silence. "Back you go."

He tucked the photo back into the diary and looked around at the mess he had made. With a grimace, he began to repack everything.

———

It was there! Below it lay an open window, its warm light pouring out into the empty street. In the room sat its prey. Perhaps some dim memory flared at the sight of the small, open book on the floor. But its mind was filled with hunger. Soon it would feed. Soon it would be free. It swept through the open window.

———

Ryan heard a soft flapping and turned his head toward the window. A woman's face, twisted with madness, hung in the frame. Trailing

behind her head like a nightmarish kite was a tangle of bloody guts.

Ryan's mind seemed to melt into a white void. He never noticed the similarity between the dripping head and the old black-and-white photo.

The Stranger

ora was watching the news with her parents and younger brother, Max. She had a "current events" assignment due at the end of the week, and she was still searching for something interesting to write about.

But even though her eyes were focused on the television screen, her mind definitely was not. She was trying to remember something that had happened earlier that day.

"Wow!" erupted Max, bringing her attention suddenly back into the room. "Hey Dora, look at that!"

The voice of the announcer swam into Dora's head as she studied the picture.

". . . over 100 vehicles involved, making this one of the worst pileups in this state's history. We go now to. . . ."

Dora stared at the images of smashed and mangled cars filling the screen. The on-the-spot reporter was pointing to a smoldering truck, burned so fiercely that its aluminum siding ran like water down its side. In the background, fire fighters and rescue crews moved eerily through a fog of windblown dust.

Dora could hear the screams of people in pain, and the shriek of a saw blade cutting into metal as paramedics tried to cut someone free from the twisted wreckage.

"Oh, no," her dad said. "That dummy left the mike open. We're not supposed to hear things like that on television!"

"Can you believe it?" asked Max, whirling around to stare at his sister. "They said the crash covers nearly a mile!"

"How about that for your project?" her father asked Dora. "Something about the way dust storms are caused, and how to prevent them from interfering with modern life?"

Dora thought about it a moment. "I don't know, Dad. That sounds more like a science project."

"You mean it sounds like too much work," her father corrected, smiling.

"How about a story about how many people get killed by nature?" Max suggested. "You could talk about earthquakes and fires. Maybe you could even get some cool pictures of bodies and stuff!"

"That's gross," Dora said.

"Wimp," countered Max. Dora ignored him, and he turned back to the television.

By the end of the night, Dora was trying to figure out a way to combine both her father's and Max's ideas. She was still puzzling over it as she went to bed.

But when she arrived at school the next morning, all her concerns about the project were swept away by her friend Valerie.

"Did you hear?" Valerie practically jumped at Dora when she got off the bus.

"What?"

"Mrs. Perle disappeared last night. There's no class today!"

"What!? Are you serious?"

Valerie's head bobbed up and down. "Yeah. They're trying to find a substitute teacher, but they couldn't get one for today."

"What happened to Mrs. Perle?"

Valerie shrugged. "Nobody knows. Or nobody's saying. Either way the result's the same!"

Dora shook her head in disbelief, and the two girls walked to the front playground. It was a warm morning, and the playground was filled with kids being dropped off by their parents.

Dora looked around the parking lot and suddenly stopped and grabbed her friend's arm.

"What?" asked Valerie, jerking around.

"You see that guy over there? By the front gate?" Dora pointed to a group of adults standing at the gate to the school.

Valerie looked where Dora pointed. "Who? The guy with the brown hat?"

"No! Next to Mrs. Rinter. See? Him! He's going back outside!"

Valerie looked but saw no one. She turned to her friend and shrugged. "Sorry. What about him?"

Dora sighed in exasperation. "I was wondering if you knew who he was. He looked familiar, but I don't know from where."

Valerie looked again toward the gate.

"He's gone now!" Dora said in exasperation. She frowned, then walked toward the swings. "It doesn't matter. Come on, let's find out what's going on today."

Valerie shrugged again and followed her friend.

They spent most of the day on the playground with the rest of their class. Dora felt sorry for Mrs. Perle, but still had one of the most fun days at school in a long time. By the end of the day she was pleasantly exhausted.

The bus dropped her off about two blocks

away from her house, with two other kids, Nigel and Dwayne.

"So what do you think happened to Mrs. Perle?" she asked Dwayne as they walked.

"Murdered," he announced. "Positively. Probably find her hacked up into tiny bits."

Nigel nodded. "Yeah, she's probably stuffed into a trash bag in the trunk of a car."

Dora rolled her eyes as the two boys tried to top each other with grisly details. Then she saw something out of the corner of her eye.

It was the man she had seen at school. He was standing at the end of the street behind them. Dora couldn't see his face, but he was tall and thin with short grey hair. He was very pale and looked even more so in contrast with the long, black coat he wore. Dora swallowed and turned away when she saw he *was* watching her.

"Nigel," she said in a low voice. "Dwayne. Do you see that guy back there at the corner?"

Before she could warn them to be careful, they both spun around and stared down the street.

"What are you talking about?" Dwayne asked in an accusing tone.

Dora turned also, but the man was no longer there.

"There was a guy standing there!" she insisted. "Tall and skinny with white hair. Dressed in black."

Nigel's eyes widened. "The murderer!"

Dwayne punched the other boy in the arm. "In the middle of the day? Don't be an idiot!"

This led to another argument, which Dora ignored. She kept glancing over her shoulder the rest of the way home, but did not see the strange man again. Nor could she remember where she had first seen him.

She was going to bring him up that night at dinner, but her parents decided it would be fun if they all went out to a movie. Dora was stunned, and Max was so surprised he became a little less obnoxious than usual. But they took advantage of the event and were in the car before their parents could change their minds.

The movie, *Galaxies Are Colliding*, was showing at the mall. The theater was practically empty, but the movie was really good. Dora loved every minute of it. In fact, she thought to herself, if it weren't for that creepy guy, this would have been a great day!

Dora tried to figure out what was going on with the strange man. "Okay," she told herself. "So why is this guy following me? Do I know him? Do I know his daughter? Why doesn't he ever change his clothes? Who is he? Where have I seen him before?"

The questions swirled so fast in her head she felt dizzy and had to give up.

After the movie, Dora's mom declared that it was still early. She somehow persuaded Dora's dad to take Max to the game store while she and Dora went shopping. Her dad actually agreed, and Dora and her mom started poking through the stores.

She was looking through the bookstore while her mom was across the way at a clothes store. And then she saw him again!

He was close this time. He looked like he was sixty or more, but what made Dora shiver was the fact that he was still wearing the same dark overcoat. She now saw that he was wearing black pants and a black shirt as well. He leaned against a pillar across from the bookstore and watched her.

Dora couldn't believe it. She ducked behind a display of books and poked her head around the side.

He *was* watching her! With a gasp, she pulled her head back and looked frantically around the store. She spotted one of the clerks and ran over to him.

"Excuse me," she began, holding her voice steady.

The clerk was a young man, and he smiled at her. "Yes?"

"I've lost my mom, and there's a strange man following me!"

The clerk became instantly serious. "Are you sure?"

Dora nodded, and the young man took her to the cashier's booth. He picked up a phone and dialed mall security, while Dora snuck a peek out at the main floor.

The man was still there. He stared into her wide eyes and smiled. Dora felt as if a lion would smile the same way at a lamb. With a gasp, she grabbed the clerk's arm.

"There he is!" she pointed.

The clerk said something into the phone and looked up. "Where?"

"Over by the pillar," Dora began, and then stopped abruptly. The man was gone again. She felt as if an ice cube had slid down her spine.

"Who?" the clerk was asking, looking at the crowd in the mall.

Fear enveloped her. Like fog, it crept into the paths and alleys of her brain. She couldn't answer.

Suddenly her mother was in front of her, with her father and brother right behind. Her dad was talking to the store clerk and an older guy dressed in a uniform.

"Are you all right?" her mother was asking.

Dora shook herself out of her strange paralysis. "I guess so." Then she looked around frantically. "Mom! Dad! There's some guy following me! I saw him a couple of times today, and just now over there." She pointed to the pillar where she had seen the stranger.

"Yeah, right," muttered Max, earning a glare from their mom.

"What did he look like?" her dad asked as he knelt down in front of her.

Dora described the man, and the security guard began talking into his walkie-talkie. Her dad stood up, thanked the store clerk, and reached protectively for Dora's arm.

"Come on," he said. "Let's go home."

Dora stared at all the faces passing by, but didn't see the man again. They made it out to the car, and she and Max piled into the backseat.

They made their way down the ramp of the parking structure to the streetlight at the bottom. Dora felt hot and cold at the same time, and couldn't stop shivering. Her chest hurt when she breathed, and her head was pounding. Her whole body felt numb.

Who was he? she wanted to scream. And finally, she felt the beginning of a memory tickle the back of her mind.

They pulled out and began driving home. Dora's brows drew together as she tried to concentrate. She knew she had seen him before he had ruined the best day she'd ever had.

But before she could make the memory come

forward, she saw him once more. They were stopped at a traffic light. Dora thought he must be crazy, because he was standing in the middle of the intersection, right in front of their car!

"That's him, Dad!" she yelled, pointing.

"Where?" her father asked, swinging his head from side to side.

Dora thought she was scared before, but her father's question seemed to freeze the blood in her veins. "He . . . he's right there," she stuttered in a small voice. Dora's heart beat frantically against her ribs as her eyes met the man's. The stranger watched her with a smile. And Dora figured she was losing her mind because now the smile seemed sad.

"Dora," her dad began before his voice faded away.

And at last Dora knew where she had seen the man before. It was on the night of the crash. The crash she had imagined herself watching on television. The crash that had crumpled the front of their car like a soda can under the rear bumper of a huge truck, and pulverized her parents in seconds.

Her vision swam, and she could hear the screams of people in pain. She heard the shriek of a saw blade cutting into metal by her head as firemen tried to cut her from the wreckage. Tears leaked from her eyes as she realized that she had lived that wonderful day only in her mind.

Her entire body hurt as she turned her head to see Max crumpled against the window, unmoving. She coughed and blood splattered on Max's still face. She didn't think the firemen were going to get to her in time.

Then the stranger somehow stood in the middle of the seat between her and Max. Incredibly, he was partly in and partly out of the car. His silver hair glowed in the moonlight as he bent down to lift Dora. And she finally knew who the dark stranger was.

School Games

Hey, Chunk," Brent whispered in the ear of the large boy sitting in front of him. "Wanna play Lone Survivor after class?"

Chuck nodded yes without turning around. Brent leaned back and flashed the thumbs-up sign across to Patrick and Dan. Then he concentrated once more on the textbook spread open in front of him.

Finally the bell rang, and another day of class vanished behind Brent and his friends. They pushed their way through the jam of kids, tossed their books into Brent's locker, and raced to the school's back playground.

"Why are we running?" Chuck panted as he struggled to keep up with the others. It was his size that had earned him the nickname "Chunk."

"Because, Chunk," Patrick answered over his shoulder, "if we don't get to the bars first, we'll never get on."

"What's the point of being in sixth grade if you can't boss other kids around?" Chuck grumbled as he kept jogging.

The school had two playgrounds—front and rear. Off to one side of the rear playground was a set of metal bars that resembled a ladder curved into an arch, with both ends set into the ground. These bars were in the middle of a sand pit.

The four friends reached the bars before anyone else. Without stopping for breath, they scrambled onto the top of the arch.

"There," said Brent, finally able to rest. "Now it's ours. You guys ready?"

Lone Survivor was a game Brent had made up. Basically, the boys had to hang by their hands from the bars while trying to knock the others loose. The last one on the bars was the winner—the lone survivor.

Sometimes they carried water over from the drinking fountains to make mud, or scattered rocks under the bars, to make the game more interesting. Once they had carried horse manure from the school stables and strewn it over the sand underneath the bars. As fun and terrifying as that had been, all four of them had gotten pretty severely punished when their parents picked them up that night. Patrick had been forced to ride home in the back of his father's truck.

"Okay," Dan said. He gripped the bars and lowered himself to hang from them. The other three did the same, and the game began.

Chuck usually won the first game or two because his greater size and power helped him to knock the other boys off. But his extra weight quickly made him tired, and then it was anybody's game.

It was a quiet afternoon, and none of the other kids even came near the sand pit. After a few rounds, the four friends regrouped at the top of the bars.

"We need to make this more difficult," said Brent after a moment.

"How about if the first person to fall stays there and tries to grab the guys on the bars?" suggested Dan.

"Nah," said Patrick scornfully. "Use your imagination." He dropped his voice and leaned closer to the others. "Picture this. For years, the hideous sand demon has slept in the sand beneath these bars. But now it's awake . . . and it's hungry."

"Why is it awake now?" Brent asked.

"The hole in the ozone layer?" Dan volunteered.

"No, no," Patrick shook his head. "It's been hibernating. It wakes up every hundred years. Anyway, the sand demon has the front half of a lizard with two clawed feet, a lizard head, and a mouth filled with rows of sharp teeth. But the back half is like a fish, so it can swim through the sand like a great white shark moves through water."

"Okay," agreed Chuck. "So what?"

"So from now on, anybody who falls has been eaten by the sand demon. They have to bury themselves in sand until the end of the game."

"Sounds good to me," said Brent. "Prepare to defend yourselves!"

He dropped from his seat and swung from his hands. Chuck clambered over a couple of rungs and did the same. Patrick and Dan dropped down next to Brent and immediately attacked him by wrapping their legs around his waist.

Chuck swung one rung closer and froze, staring at the sand. "Hey, guys?" he said in a quavering voice.

The other three stopped. "What's wrong, Chunk?" asked Dan.

"I just saw the sand move," Chuck said. He stared at the rippled surface below them.

"It's the sand demon!" Brent cried, laughing. With two quick overhand swings, Patrick broke away from Dan and Brent and pushed at Chuck with his legs.

Chuck gave a startled yell and launched a wild attack. Patrick hadn't expected Chuck to have so much energy this late in the match, and before he knew it, his hands had slipped from the bars.

Patrick hit the ground with a thump. He lay there a moment, catching his breath, then rolled over and pointed at Chuck. "You'll pay for that, you scum," he promised in mock anger.

Before Chuck could reply, the sand erupted next to Patrick. A black-and-tan creature shot into the air like a dolphin leaping out of the ocean. The lizard head opened its mouth to reveal glistening white rows of triangular teeth and a forked tongue that darted madly about.

Patrick screamed so loudly that his face seemed to twist. The others hung there in shock as the creature raked one huge claw across Patrick's face, leaving raw flesh and white bone. Then it dropped on top of Patrick's body and sank back into the sand.

Brent realized he was still trying to scream, but no sound was coming from his raw throat. He looked at Chuck, who was staring down through his feet at the bloody sand. Dan was desperately pulling himself into a sitting position on top of the bars.

Brent swung one leg up over the bars and began to lever himself up onto the top. "Chunk," Brent croaked. "Get up." Chuck still hadn't moved, so Brent and Dan crawled over to him and tugged on his arms.

Chuck gasped and looked up, almost losing his grip on the bars. The other boys grabbed his hands.

"Don't fall," Dan rasped. "Get up here."

Chuck seemed to come to his senses and struggled to raise himself to the top of the bars. After a moment, all three were perched like sitting ducks.

"Patrick," Chuck said, and tears began to fill his wide eyes. "Did you see his face? It was ripped off! But he was still screaming! He was still alive when that thing took him down!" Chuck's voice kept rising until he was practically yelling. Tears poured down his cheeks.

"Chunk!" Dan snapped. "Stop it! We saw it, too!" He shuddered. He had also seen Patrick's jaw muscles working, trying to beg for help through a mouth that had been ripped to shreds. He shook himself.

"What the heck was that?" Dan asked out loud. "Where did it come from?"

Brent cleared his throat. "I don't know," he was able to say clearly even though his throat still felt sore. "But it appeared right after Patrick told us about it."

Dan stared at him. "What do you mean? That Patrick somehow summoned this thing? Are you crazy?"

"I don't know," Brent said again. He tried to hold back the tears he felt threatening to surge forth. "It just seems pretty strange that it just shows up all of a sudden!"

"We have to get out of here," Chuck interrupted.

"Yeah, sure," said Dan. "How? Fly?"

"We can jump to the asphalt," Brent said.

Chuck gulped and looked around. The sand pit was bordered by the asphalt of the playground. But it had never looked as far away as it did right at that moment.

As the three boys studied the distance, the sand underneath the bars shifted like something was moving just under the surface. The pool of blood had sunk into the sand, leaving no trace of Patrick.

"Oh great," Chuck said. "Looks like it's finished its Patrick snack and wants to have dinner now!"

"Don't think about it," warned Brent hoarsely. "Concentrate on jumping over it to the asphalt."

"If I don't try now," Dan said, "I'm never going to make it." He lowered himself until he was hanging by his arms. He began to swing back and forth. He gathered momentum and mentally prepared himself to release the bars.

With terrifying speed, the monster leaped up out of the sand. Brent heard a tearing sound and saw the creature drop back to the sand. He looked down at Dan, feeling his stomach heave.

It had happened so fast that Dan was still holding onto the bars. But everything below his waist was gone, and blood poured out onto the sand below. Even as Brent's stomach began to empty, Dan's brain realized he was dead and his hands slipped off the bars. The rest of his body hit the ground and was sucked under by the creature.

Sounds filtered slowly back into Brent's head. He could hear Chuck crying and pleading for his mom and dad. Brent felt tears burn his eyes as he swung his head up and wiped his mouth.

"Chunk. We've got to try something else."

"Oh, yeah," Chuck sobbed. "No problem." Brent could see that Chuck was about to lose it.

"Chunk," Brent said. He crawled over to his last friend and shook his leg. "Chunk. We don't know how high that thing can jump. We have to get off these bars."

"How, Brent?" Chuck wailed.

"We gotta think it away."

Chuck's face twisted as he laughed and cried at the same time. Brent began to be afraid for his friend's sanity. *"Think* it away? What are you talking about?"

Brent turned and looked across the sand. Ten feet to the asphalt, he guessed; maybe more, maybe less.

"Somehow, Patrick imagined this monster into existence. Our only chance is to imagine it gone, and then jump for the asphalt."

Chuck slowly lifted his head to look at Brent. "Dan was right," he said quietly. "You are crazy."

With a chill, Brent suddenly realized it could be true—he could have totally lost his mind in these last few minutes.

"We've got to try, Chunk," Brent insisted. "What other choice do we have? Come on. It's gone. Just keep saying it—it's gone. It's gone. It's gone."

Chuck joined in the chant for a few minutes then suddenly scrunched up his face. "I can't do it. I keep thinking about Patrick and Dan!"

The pebbled skin of the creature's back showed briefly above the sand as it prowled under the bars.

"Chunk," Brent was desperate. "Try harder! If we can imagine it gone, just for a moment, we can jump to the asphalt!"

They sat there silently, trying to save themselves by not thinking about the monster. After a moment, Chuck nodded grimly.

Without waiting for second thoughts Brent got to his feet and held his arms out for balance. He took a couple of deep breaths. Then, feeling like he moved in slow motion, he squatted down as far as he could and launched himself into the air like a strange bird.

He had a brief glimpse of the sand pit, then the asphalt was rushing up to slam him in the shoulder. His right knee pounded against the asphalt as he rolled to a stop and lay there—breath knocked out, scraped, and battered. But he had made it!

He gathered himself to his feet and turned to face Chuck. "Okay, Chunk," he called. "Piece of cake! Now it's your turn!"

Chuck began shaking his head. "I can't," he said in a voice so low Brent barely heard it. "I can't do it."

"Chunk!" Brent yelled. "The monster is gone, right? As long as you know the monster is gone, you can do it!" He watched anxiously as Chuck sat there. Then, moving as if there was no hope in the world, Chuck dropped to the sand.

"You can do it, man!" Brent yelled. "The monster's gone!"

Chuck pushed himself to his feet and started running across the sand. Brent sucked in a breath and held it as Chuck approached. In a flash it was over, and Chuck stood next to Brent on the safety of the asphalt.

For a moment, Brent couldn't believe it was over. Then he couldn't help himself, he began to laugh. Chuck looked at him strangely.

"Sorry, Chunk," Brent wheezed. He forced himself to stop laughing. "It's just that I really didn't think it would work."

"What?" Chuck cried.

"Never mind. Let's get out of here." He put an arm around Chuck's shoulder to help support his weight.

"Thank God Patrick didn't give the thing four legs," Brent said as they limped away. "Can you imagine that?" Chuck nodded silently.

The sand demon pulled itself out of the sand behind them. It was able to walk quite well on its two new, powerful hind legs. It seemed to grin as it moved quickly behind the two boys.

On the Radio

allie watched her dad struggle to unload the old Motorola radio from the back of his truck.

"Where's this one going to go, Dad?" she asked.

"Don't know," he grunted. "Garage for now."

Hallie looked at her mom, who smiled and rolled her eyes. Hallie's dad couldn't resist collecting old radios and fixing them. But there were always some that couldn't be repaired, so they ended up in the garage. With all the radios in there now, there was barely room for the car. With this latest addition, it looked to Hallie that the car might actually lose out.

"Where'd you get it, Dad?" she asked as he frog-walked the heavy radio over to his workbench.

With a sigh, he set the huge console down. "Auction. This antique store was cleaning out its old inventory, and—"

"You picked it up for a song," Hallie's mom finished the old joke.

Hallie's dad smiled and shrugged. "What more can I say?" He began unscrewing the back panel of the radio.

Hallie's mom laughed and went back inside the house. Hallie kissed her dad good-bye and went over to a friend's house.

That night at the dinner table she asked her dad how the new radio sounded.

"Not good," he said dejectedly. "In fact, I'm not sure I can get it to work. The rhadometer is fused; and even if I could find a replacement, the Wesley coils are completely gone. Missing!" He shook his head and glumly stuck another bite of dinner into his mouth.

The next day, as her dad set off on a search for the missing parts, Hallie went to take a look at his latest buy. She was beginning to appreciate old radios, and this one was certainly a beauty.

It stood nearly two feet high and was made of satiny, richly grained walnut. The black mesh screen looked almost new behind the carved speaker window. The ivory knobs and channel buttons were worn smooth and yellowish white. The glass dial was so clear that the black channel numbers seemed to be floating in space.

Hallie ran her fingers across the glossy finish on the front. She felt sorry for her dad—this would have been a nice radio to have working. She twisted the power dial and felt the soft click of connection.

With growing surprise, she watched as the dial began to glow with a warm yellow light. A faint hum grew into words coming from the speaker.

" *. . . not sure I want to be here when she does.* " The swelling music marked a pause in the drama that was being broadcast, but Hallie didn't wait to hear the station identification. She ran into the house, calling for her mother.

"Mom!" she shouted when her mother looked up from the book she was reading. "Mom! Dad's radio is working!"

"Is he back already?"

"No! I mean, it's working all by itself. I turned it on, and it just started working!"

Hallie's mother got to her feet and followed Hallie out to the garage. Hallie jerked to a stop when she saw that the radio was silent, its dial dark and dusty.

Hallie darted over and began turning the power knob back and forth. Although she could still feel the little click when the radio should have turned on, nothing happened.

"It really was working, Mom," she insisted.

Her mother just watched her with a raised eyebrow.

Hallie's shoulders slumped after a few more tries. "Well, I don't know why, but it's not working now."

"Maybe we should leave it for your father to figure out," her mother suggested. She patted Hallie on the shoulder and went back inside the house.

Hallie stared at the radio. "You stupid box," she muttered. Defiantly, she flicked the power knob one last time.

The dial lit up instantly, and the program came through loud and clear. Hallie felt a small shock send her skin rustling as she stared at the speaker.

On impulse, she glanced over her shoulder while keeping an eye on the radio. "Mom," she called. "Mom, could you come here please?"

"What is it, Hallie?" her mother shouted back. "I'm on the phone!"

Hallie was about to answer when she realized how silly she would sound. "Never mind," she said. She stepped closer to the radio and peered behind.

Jolts of fear surged through her at the simple sight of the plug laying on the bench—there was no power going to the radio at all! She rocked back on her heels and stared at the dial.

"This is impossible," she whispered, trying to calm herself.

She became suddenly aware of the program that was on. It was some weepy drama about a young girl who had been in a car wreck and was in the hospital.

"Please tell us the truth, doctor," a man's voice pleaded. *"Will our little girl be all right?"*

The doctor sighed. *"I'm just not sure. You must understand—she went through the front windshield face-first. She's suffered incredible lacerations of her face and neck."*

"You mean she'll be disfigured?" the mother broke in, nearly hysterical.

"No," said the doctor. *"Probably not. But there is a chance that she has lost both her voice and her sight."*

"What are you doing, Hallie?" her mother asked.

Hallie jumped. She started to answer, but her mouth hung open as she realized that she was sitting on the floor of the garage, even though she could not remember having sat down. She gestured to the radio, but it was dead again.

Hallie gathered her thoughts. "I'm uh . . . nothing, Mom. Just sitting here thinking."

Her mother studied her. "Are you sure you're all right? You had an odd expression on your face. Like you were listening to something."

Hallie shook her head. "No, I'm okay. I was just daydreaming."

"Okay," her mother smiled, unconvinced. "I came to see if you wanted some lunch." Hallie nodded and got stiffly to her feet.

She was quiet during lunch, thinking of the program. It was weird—she didn't really like soap operas and stuff like that, but she couldn't wait to get back out to the garage to listen to the radio.

She wolfed down her food, thanked her mother, and went back outside. The buttons of the radio grinned at her from under the single eye of the dial. Suddenly her hand was moving on its own, and she turned the power on. The same show purred on, and Hallie slowly sank to the cold cement floor, ignoring the world around her as she got lost in the drama.

After a while—she didn't know how long—the radio suddenly stopped. Daylight was leaking away from the sky outside the garage. The headlights of her father's truck swept across the lawn as he pulled into the driveway.

Hallie pushed herself to her feet. Her dad turned off the engine and climbed out.

"Hallie!" he called in surprise. "What are you doing out here?" He walked over to her.

Hallie's mouth opened, but her voice barely croaked out. She cleared her throat, swallowed, and tried again. "I think your radio's working," she rasped.

Her father looked at her with concern. "Are you feeling okay? Your voice sounds pretty bad. Not coming down with a cold are you?"

"I don't know," she answered in her scratchy voice. "I guess maybe I am."

"It wouldn't surprise me," her father said, "if you've been sitting on that cold floor for a while." He put his arm around her shoulders. "So, what about that old monster?" he waved at the silent radio.

Hallie wanted to explain about the lit dial with no power, but she was suddenly unable to put it into words. "I was wondering if you found any parts?" she asked instead.

"None," he said with surprising good cheer. "I really got taken by that dealer. Apparently, this model doesn't even exist! Mr. Kaplan said it must be a homemade job—bits and pieces from other radios." Her dad chuckled. "No wonder I'd never seen anything like it."

He picked Hallie up and swung her around, and they went inside. She took one last glance over her shoulder at the dark radio. Something her father had said should have scared her, but all she felt was empty.

She couldn't seem to keep her attention on her dinner. The food seemed tasteless and dry.

"Are you all right, dear?" her mother asked finally.

"I'm not sure, Mom. Maybe I'm getting sick." She finished poking at her food and went upstairs to bed.

That night she dreamt of the radio. Images from the drama she had been listening to filled her mind—the convalescing girl, the worried parents, and some old man that must be the

grandfather telling the girl he would do anything to help her get better.

"You've got to believe me, sweets," the old man promised in his rough voice. *"No matter what I have to do, I'll make sure you get better."*

In Hallie's dream, the old man then turned toward her and grabbed her by the throat, screaming, *"You'll help us, won't you?"*

In the morning, Hallie's voice was worse. When she greeted her parents at the breakfast table, her faint, reedy voice was so alarming that her mother rushed her straight back to bed.

"I feel okay, Mom," Hallie protested hoarsely. "I've just got some laryngitis."

"Maybe," her mother said. "Maybe not. You can't expect me to believe you're upset about missing a day of school!"

Hallie smiled. "No, I guess not."

Her mother fussed over her some more, then went to get ready for work. Her dad came and kissed her good-bye and was soon followed by her mother.

"If you need anything, give me a call at work, okay?"

"I will Mom," Hallie whispered, her voice nearly gone. "See you later."

Her parents had barely pulled out of the driveway before Hallie was out of bed. The need to listen to the radio was filling her up, driving her forward. Without bothering to put anything over her nightshirt, she padded barefoot out to the cold garage.

The radio waited on the workbench for her. This time it turned on as she entered the room. She listened to the same program.

The little girl on the program was still in the hospital, but she was starting to recover. Her mother and father were at her bedside, and the mother was crying as her daughter spoke for the first time since the accident.

"I'm okay, Mom," she breathed in a voice that sounded strangely familiar to Hallie.

"Oh, honey," the mother cried. *"We were so worried about you. Your grandfather said you'd be all right, but I don't know how he knew, and I . . . ,"* the woman began sobbing in relief.

"Please don't cry, Mom," the girl whispered.

Hallie recognized the girl's voice now. It was Hallie's voice! She felt a vague warning stirring in the back of her mind, but ignored it. Instead, she leaned forward to stare at the dial. It seemed like her vision was very blurry today. She had trouble focusing on the radio.

"Everything will be all right," the girl promised her mother. *"In fact, I think my sight is beginning to return, too."*

Talk to the Animals

○T○

Don't forget my class is going to the zoo today," Todd said to his mom and dad at the breakfast table.

"I thought Mr. Fagan was out this week?" his mom asked, looking up from the front page she was reading.

"He is. But they got a substitute."

"I pity that person," his mom said, smiling.

"Better have a good look while you're there," his dad said from behind his newspaper. "Apparently the zoo is having trouble raising money."

"Does that mean they're going to close?" his mother asked.

"Probably not. But they may have to sell some animals and they won't have any way to replace them. Anyway, they certainly won't be adding any new species for a while."

"Gotta go," said Todd as he slurped the last of his cereal. "The bus is supposed to be leaving at nine."

He raced upstairs to brush his teeth and get his day pack. Then he raced back downstairs. "Bye, Mom! Bye, Dad!" he called as he slammed the door shut behind him. He wheeled his bicycle out of the garage and pumped hard toward school.

The rest of his classmates were already lining up at the bus when Todd rode up. He locked his bike, jumped on the bus, and forced his way to the back to sit by his friends, Blake and Curtis. The substitute teacher, Ms. Millet, was sitting at the front of the bus, trying desperately to remember names with the help of Ms. Cox, the bus driver.

When the bus finally pulled up in the zoo's parking lot, the teacher had all the kids line up in two rows. Then she marched them to the ticket window and got everyone admitted. Once inside, Ms. Cox took one group and Ms. Millet, the other.

Todd and Curtis ended up in the group led by Ms. Millet. Much to their dismay, she chose the bird aviary to visit first.

"This is pretty lame," Todd sulked to Curtis as

their class wandered through the huge, noisy bird cage.

"Yeah," agreed his friend. "What's next, the petting zoo?"

As far as Todd was concerned, the day never quite recovered after that. It was fun making faces at the monkeys and laughing at their resemblance to furry little people. And Ms. Millet took them to see a lion-taming show, which was cool. But she also forced them to take the dumb little train that practically crawled around the park, and Todd just hoped nobody else saw them.

They stopped for lunch with the other half of the class. Blake, who had been with the group led by Ms. Cox, came over to Todd and Curtis.

"How's it going?" he asked his two friends.

"Don't ask," said Curtis. "What have you guys been doing?"

"It's been great! When we were at the Reptile House, I saw this big old snake suck a mouse down whole!"

Todd looked at Curtis grimly.

"Then," Blake continued, "we went to the Marine Exhibit and the African Section and...."

Todd stopped listening after a moment. Sometimes Blake could really get on his nerves.

After lunch Ms. Millet finally took them to the

Reptile House. Todd and Curtis watched the enormous serpents slowly coiling and uncoiling around the tree branches.

"I wonder what this place is like at night," Todd murmured.

"Must be kind of busy," Curtis guessed. "There are probably guys cleaning cages and sweeping up and stuff."

"Yeah, but that's probably when they feed all the animals, too," Todd whispered excitedly. "Wouldn't that be cool to watch! I wonder if they toss live animals to the lions so they can practice their hunting?"

Curtis shrugged, and they moved on to the next glass window. But as they stared at the lizards, Todd found himself imagining the zoo at night. Would it be like the jungle? Dark except for a few pools of light . . . the cries of the night birds, the sounds of the other nocturnal animals, and the snarls of the lions as they tore into their nightly dinner? It sounded better by the minute.

"Hey," he said to Curtis. "What do you say we have our own field trip?"

"What do you mean?"

"Let's come back here after closing! We could sneak in and watch the zookeeper feed the animals and stuff like that."

Curtis' eyes widened. "Are you serious? How would we get away with that?"

"Easy. When we get back to school, you call your parents and tell them you're spending the night at my house. Then I call my parents and tell them I'm spending the night at *your* house. Since it's Friday night, I know I can talk my mom and dad into it. Then we hop on our bikes and come straight back here."

Curtis didn't say anything, but Todd could tell he was hooked.

"Come on," Todd pleaded. "My dad said the zoo was probably going to close soon 'cause they're running out of money. This'll be something we can tell everyone about for the rest of our lives!"

The rest of the afternoon passed in a blur to Todd. The more he thought about what they were planning the more he couldn't wait to go back to school. Finally, the bus pulled into the school parking lot. Todd and Curtis ran for the phones to put their plan into action. Moments later they were on their bikes and heading back to the zoo.

They stopped a couple of blocks away and chained their bikes to a rack in a park playground. They goofed around until the sun had almost set, then they cautiously made their way to the zoo perimeter fence and climbed quickly over it into the parking lot.

Darting over to a parked zoo trolley, they

wriggled under it on their stomachs. A number of trolleys were parked side by side, so they were able to squirm along under them—crossing almost the entire length of the employee parking lot without being seen. After they reached the other end, they sprinted out from under the last trolley and into the employee entrance.

They were back in the zoo. Everything seemed so different in the cool, dim evening. The shadows cast by the walkway lights distorted the trees and cages and created a spooky atmosphere.

"Where to first?" Curtis whispered.

"Beats me. How about the Reptile House?"

Curtis shrugged and followed Todd. On their way, they passed a trail that they hadn't explored during the day. Todd stopped to peer at the sign on the lamppost.

"Animal Acquisitions," Todd read. "Hospital and Nursery."

"Where are you going?" Curtis asked as Todd veered down the new path.

"Come on. Let's see what's down here."

The trail wound along behind many of the cages in the African section, but there weren't any displays or animals along its length. Suddenly, they turned a bend to face a building. Long and low, it looked like it was made of solid concrete. There were no windows, and only one light was on by the steel door.

"That must be where all the babies and sick animals are kept," Todd said. "Let's go check it out. Maybe we can pet a baby tiger or something."

Curtis rolled his eyes but followed his friend. Sticking to the shadows, they snuck closer to the building. They watched the door for at least ten minutes but nobody came out.

The clear space in front of the building extended around the side, and Todd went that way. They came upon a large metal door, and next to it was a window with faint light spilling out. The two boys scurried over under the window and peered in on what looked like one big room. Tables stood in the middle of the room, covered with glass beakers and containers, surgical implements, scraps of paper, and objects that they couldn't figure out.

To their left and directly under the window were some desks with computer consoles, and these were also cluttered. Across the room from them, two long glass cages formed an "L" in the corner.

The light was coming from the glass cages. Todd and Curtis could see tiny moving shapes behind the glass.

"I told you," Todd said as he poked Curtis. "The babies! Come on." He slid open the window and pulled himself inside.

"Wait," Curtis began, then took a deep breath and followed. He squirmed through the window and closed it behind him. The floor of the room was covered with linoleum tiles, like a hospital. Todd smiled and began walking over to the cages.

Suddenly, the floor to the left of the front door began to move! Without thinking, the two boys threw themselves under a desk to hide.

The moving section of floor was a trap door. The outline of it was hidden by the placement of the floor tiles, and Todd didn't think he would have ever known it was there if it hadn't opened.

They watched in fascination as a man in a lab coat climbed up from what was obviously a basement room. He dropped the trap door shut, unlocked the front door, and left. Then they heard him lock the door from the outside.

Todd turned to Curtis with wide eyes. "Did you see that?"

"Of course! What was it?"

"I don't know. But I'm going to find out!"

Todd scrambled to his feet and went over to the trap door. But even now that he knew it was there, he didn't know how it operated. He looked around at the walls.

"I don't think this is a good idea," Curtis attempted.

Todd lunged forward and grabbed the loose edge of one of the tiles. The floor swung up to reveal stairs going down. "Wow! This is unreal!" said Todd, his face flushed.

They crept down the stairs and entered a well-lit corridor. The smell of wild animals washed over them. "Maybe there's something really rare down here," Todd whispered. Curtis nodded, but didn't look too sure.

They inched along the corridor toward an open door. When they reached it, Todd slowly edged his face around the corner.

It was another room, similar to the one upstairs. It was just as large, but cages lined all the walls. A table was in the middle of the room with straps and syringes piled on top. There was also a strange-looking gun. One fluorescent light lit the room.

The cages were fairly big, and Todd could see a tiger with its back to him in one of them. The others held large furry animals, but he couldn't tell what kind. Todd tiptoed as close as he dared to the tiger's cage and tried to see if there were any cubs.

Suddenly, the tiger rolled over. Todd's chest stopped moving as he struggled to breathe. Curtis gasped, too, as he saw the thing in the cage.

It wasn't a tiger. Or at least, not all tiger. It had the body of a tiger, but its front legs looked like enormous, muscular human arms, and its head was a hideous cross between a cat and a woman. It stared at Todd and Curtis, then abruptly lunged at them, shooting an arm between the bars and grabbing the front of Todd's shirt.

Todd screamed and tore himself free. He jumped back and knocked into Curtis, sending them both sprawling. The other animals heard the commotion and pressed against the bars of their cages.

Todd looked wildly around at the nightmarish creatures watching him. Half-human, half-animal, some with just enough humanity left to make Todd shudder. Others looked like horribly deformed people, and Todd felt his stomach do a slow roll.

"What the . . . " Curtis tried to speak but couldn't.

"We gotta get out of here," Todd announced shakily. He began scrambling to his feet. The tiger-thing began roaring in a high-pitched, breathy voice, as if its vocal cords were still human. It threw itself against the bars of its cage, reaching with its obscene human arm through the bars.

"Jeez, Todd," Curtis finally managed to croak. "What are these things?"

"I don't know," Todd said as he backed away. A monster with a gazelle's body and the chest and face of a man was rearing up and kicking at the bars of its cage. A hunchbacked man with tusks thrusting out of his lower jaw was trying to pry the bars of his prison apart.

Todd and Curtis turned and ran back to the door, right into the arms of the white-coated man they had seen earlier.

"Can I help you?" he asked in a frighteningly calm voice, as he put his large hand around Todd's neck and a muscular arm around Curtis. Roughly, he pushed the two boys back into the room.

The creatures quieted down as soon as they saw the man. Todd struggled to get loose, and the man released him. Todd took a step and spun around to face him.

"What are those things?" he squeaked. Curtis stood there, open-mouthed.

The man chuckled. "My pets. The zoo can't afford to buy animals, but I can provide them with plenty of cheap substitutes."

"But," Curtis choked out, "they're people!"

"Oh, they were," the man admitted. He picked up a gun from the table, casually loading a dart into its chamber as he continued talking.

"Of course, its unfortunate that the brain is always the last human organ to change over to animal." He stopped. "Or maybe it never changes. I can't really say. Once the serum is injected the results are irreversible."

Todd jumped past the man and yanked open the door. Filling the short hallway was the largest alligator he had ever seen. But although it had an alligator's head and body, it stood erect on two human-shaped legs, muscular and scaled. Two massive green arms folded over its chest.

"But I'm not overly cruel," he heard the scientist say behind him. "I do try to fit personality to shape. The gentleman before you used to be a petty criminal."

There was a hiss, and Todd turned to see Curtis clutching at his neck. Then his friend fell to the floor and began shaking as if his bones were snapping inside his body. The alligator-man grabbed Todd from behind and held him tightly.

"The young lady in the tiger stripes loved cats," the scientist kept talking in his insanely calm voice. "The gentleman with the tusks ate like a pig." He laughed and fitted another dart into the gun.

"So I think you will make a nice addition to the primate collection. Monkeys are so very curious."

Todd began to scream as the scientist raised the gun and fired the dart into his chest. Pain seared through his body as a tail began tearing its way through the skin of his lower back.

Mirror Image

S ummer is the absolute worst time to move," announced Loren to her two best friends.

"Yeah," agreed Stephanie. "So what did your parents say?"

"They don't think so," Loren said with disgust. "They say it's better to move during the summer because that way I can start the school year with my new class."

"So what?" asked Natalie. "Summer's when you get to hang out with your friends, like having sleep-overs and stuff. Who cares who you'll be sitting next to in class!"

"That's what I tried to tell them, but they don't care. We're moving anyway."

"When?" asked Stephanie.

"In a week or two."

This news cast a pall over the three friends. They walked quietly through the opening-day crowds at the Wonders of the World Carnival. It had been setting up all week, and today was its grand opening—with all sorts of rides, contests, games, and shows.

But, Loren thought gloomily, this might be one of the last times she and her friends would be together. "I wish we weren't moving," she said miserably.

"But we can still see each other," reassured Stephanie.

"Sure," Natalie chimed in. "We can still come over and spend the night and stuff."

Loren wasn't convinced, but she didn't contradict her friend. Instead, she changed the subject. "What do you guys want to go on?" she asked.

"Roller coasters," Stephanie answered quickly.

"Fun House," Natalie added.

"We can't," Loren pointed out. "The sign at the front said the Fun House was closed today for some kind of cleaning."

Natalie shrugged. "Roller coasters it is."

They made it a point to go on every roller coaster at least twice, which had them all feeling a bit dizzy after a while. They took a breather and wandered through the crowds, stopping to watch a juggler or to play a game.

The fair was really crowded, and they had to stand in line for everything. They were nearing the front of the ice cream line when Natalie leaned toward the other two girls and whispered, "What's with that guy over there?"

Loren glanced across the pavement and saw a tall, overweight man—slightly dirty looking with stained pants and a torn black jacket. A few stray hairs stuck out from under his cap, and he was watching the three girls through thick glasses. He flashed a mouthful of yellowish teeth as Loren let her eyes sweep past him.

She casually turned back to her friends. "He's definitely weird looking."

"Yeah," said Natalie. "He's been watching us practically the whole time we've been in line."

"Just ignore him," Stephanie suggested.

All three of the girls tried to follow Stephanie's advice. But each time Loren sort of casually looked around, he was still standing in the same spot, watching them.

When they had all bought their ice cream, they quickly walked away, practically skipping around the corner of the building and pushing into the crowd in the open space beyond. Loren led the way, weaving in and out of the people filling the square, trying not to make a noticeable path. Natalie and Stephanie followed her closely. At the other side of the plaza Loren pretended to stop and look at a display of blown-glass sculptures.

"Is he following us?" Stephanie asked as she moved next to Loren.

"I don't know," began Natalie. Then, "There he is!"

Loren chanced a look, and the creepy guy was coming around the corner of the building. He was talking over his shoulder to another guy in blue jeans and a dirty sweatshirt. They both began heading across the small plaza toward where Loren and her friends were hiding.

Loren grabbed at Stephanie and pulled her behind the display stand. Then she spotted the open doorway of one of the attractions, and ducked inside with Stephanie in tow.

Before their eyes could adjust, Natalie came barreling in. "He's coming over here!" she panted. "He has someone with him!"

"I know," Loren snapped. "Did he see you?"

"I think so. He was heading right this way when I ran in."

Loren looked around. They were in a small room with four black-painted walls. There was nobody else in the room. Directly across from them was a door. Without thinking, she twisted the knob and flung it open. "In here!"

They piled in and Loren pulled the door shut,

locking it behind them. They stood in a corridor that went about five feet before taking an abrupt turn to the left. There were carnival mirrors on the walls, reflecting the nervous girls in grotesque shapes.

"It's the Fun House," said Stephanie.

"Are you sure he was coming this way?" Loren asked Natalie.

"Yeah, I'm sure."

Loren strode off down the corridor. When she turned she let out a gasp.

It was a mirror maze. It seemed to stretch forever, with hundreds of surprised Lorens standing in countless doorways. The whole place was faintly lit by some kind of hidden light, making it seem to glow from within the mirrored walls.

"Wow," breathed Natalie from right behind her. "This is cool!"

"Do you think he's still following us?" Stephanie asked nervously.

Before Loren could answer, the locked door rattled as someone tried the handle. "Hey, girls!" the man yelled, his voice muffled by the door. "Come on out."

"Yes," Loren answered Stephanie as she stuck her hands out in front of her. "Come on," she ordered, taking a careful step forward.

The man began pounding on the door. "Come

on, I know you're in there." He paused, then began banging again. "Hey, the ride's closed for a reason. You have to get out!"

"Yeah, right," Loren muttered as they worked their way deeper into the maze. After a couple of turns, they could no longer hear him.

Within a few more steps they were lost. Groping in front of her face for any openings in the glass, Loren led the little clump of friends. The faint illumination barely allowed her to see her hands let alone anything in front of her, making it all the more difficult to move. And it was silent, so silent Loren could hear the others breathing. Suddenly they found themselves in an open area.

"Do you think he gave up?" Stephanie asked in a low voice.

"I hope so," said Natalie, looking around. "Shouldn't there be more people in here?"

"Remember?" Loren reminded her. "The Fun House is closed today."

"Well," Natalie continued, "I say we stay right here until somebody else comes in. There's going to be cleaning crew people, right?"

"But that could be ages!" Stephanie protested.

"Yeah," agreed Natalie. "But that guy might be waiting until we come out."

"I don't feel like sitting here forever," Stephanie continued. "If Loren's right and this ride is closed, then we could be in here for an eternity!"

"Oh, calm down," Loren said. "We're not going to be in here for long!" She started exploring the dimensions of the clearing they were in.

Stephanie's head was spinning. Things had been moving too fast for her. "Let's think about this," she began. "He may not have been following us. Maybe he just happened to come in the same direction."

"Uh huh," Natalie grunted. "And maybe he just wanted to wander around this closed mirror maze and was so upset because we got here first." She slipped around a corner and disappeared from sight.

"Better stay together," warned Loren.

"Yeah, yeah," Natalie's voice floated back.

"Anyway," Stephanie continued to Loren. "All I'm trying to say is maybe we overreacted."

Loren nodded thoughtfully. "I suppose that's possible. But even so, we'll just work our way out of here and that will be that."

"Hi guys!"

Loren looked around and saw Natalie. Then, a split second later, she realized it was only a reflection. "Natalie," she called in a low voice. "Come back!"

Natalie waved. "Just a second. I thought I saw something over here."

They watched as she took a step forward. It looked to Loren as though Natalie was starting to bend down when she disappeared behind another mirror. Loren was about to say something to Stephanie when they heard a cry— quickly cut short.

Loren and Stephanie stared at each other, their eyes wide. "Natalie?" Loren called hesitantly. There was no answer. "Natalie, you're scaring us. Quit goofing around."

Stephanie began to sniffle. "What was that, Loren? What happened?"

"I don't know," Loren hissed. "We have to go see. She may have hurt herself somehow."

"What if it was *him?*" Stephanie whined, tears filling her eyes.

Loren clenched her teeth and fought the urge to hit her friend. She felt her own tears threatening to break through too. "Stop it! Come on!"

Stephanie shook her head. "I can't." She sank down into a crouch. "I'll wait here."

Loren certainly didn't want to go alone. But she had to move; she had to do something. It was as if her world had suddenly disappeared, leaving her in this wild nightmare of strange men and disappearing friends.

"All right, then. Stay right here!" Loren slowly shuffled forward, following the path Natalie had taken.

Within a turn she was alone. She could not see Stephanie, but she could hear her faint sniffling. Loren bit a knuckle and kept on moving.

Left, left, right, left, and she could see Stephanie again. She whistled softly to get her friend's attention, then waved when Stephanie looked up.

Loren took another step, and her stomach began to clench as tight as her fists. On the floor in front of her was one of Natalie's earrings. Loren bent down and gently picked it up. Still crouching, barely breathing, she turned the next corner.

Her stomach shot to the back of her throat, blocking her strangled attempts to suck air into her lungs. The floor was glistening red, and a sickeningly sweet smell hung in the air. It looked as if somebody had spilled a bucket of red paint, but Loren knew that wasn't it at all.

She fought back the nausea that kept pushing at her throat. Natalie was nowhere in sight but a trail led away from the puddle where something had been dragged along the floor.

Without thinking, Loren took a step forward. The trail led straight to a mirror and stopped. Dazed, uncomprehending, Loren ran her fingers along the cool surface of the glass. It was as if the mirror had opened up and Natalie had disappeared inside.

"Inside the mirror?" she whispered. "A secret door, maybe?" She tried to figure out what that would mean in a maze made out of mirrors, but before she could even form an idea she heard Stephanie scream. Moving clumsily around the spot where Natalie had been, Loren ran to the part of the maze that looked back on Stephanie.

And then Loren screamed, too. There, standing about as tall as Stephanie, was a horrible creature. It had black and shriveled skin like it had been burnt in some fire. Its arms and legs bent at strange angles, but it looked very muscular. Its hands ended in claws that shone like the silver mirrors around them. Its mouth hung open, and blood-red drool swung from its lips. Its teeth were glistening white fangs.

When Loren screamed it looked straight at her, and she shrank back at the hatred in its eyes. Stephanie had pushed herself up against the wall and was screaming hoarsely. Loren watched as the thing took a single step toward her friend. Then, with a negligent wave of its hand, it tore Stephanie's throat open to the spine. Blood fountained out, spraying the mirrors in tiny geysers.

Loren wished her mind would stop working. But she watched as the creature grabbed Stephanie's limp body and slung it over its shoulder. Then it walked out of sight.

Loren stood rooted to the spot. Against the horror that tried to overwhelm her, a small rational part of her brain continued to function.

But what it told her just intensified the fear. Because she knew where Stephanie had been sitting when she last saw her. And she knew that there was no opening for the creature to have disappeared through. Unless that thing was able to walk through mirrors.

Loren thought of the trail of blood that seemed to lead straight into a mirror. She thought of all the mirrors she had yet to pass to escape this maze. And that tiny working part of her mind counted down the minutes she had left to live.

Crack Up There

The crack had been in the television room for years. It started high up in the corner and creeped down where the walls joined for about four feet. It wasn't particularly wide, maybe half an inch. Really, the crack had never bothered Eugene before. Not until tonight.

His sister, Cindy, had decided that she couldn't possibly share a room with her little brother anymore. So after moving all the furniture out except the shelves against one wall, the old television room became Eugene's bedroom. At first Eugene liked having his own room. But tonight everything had changed. He had lain awake in bed for a while after his parents had wished him good night. It was strange not to have his sister to talk to or tease before going to sleep. But eventually he had drifted off.

He wasn't sure how long he had been asleep before a soft glow shone through his closed eyelids. He opened his eyes, and there was a curious light in the room. He turned over slowly, frowning, to face a faint green glow coming from the crack high up in the corner. He glanced at the window, hoping he would see the friendly globe of the moon shining through the glass. But even as he looked, he knew that moonlight couldn't cast such a strange color.

The window was dark. Eugene fixed his eyes on the strange glow as he pushed himself into a sitting position. It looked as if the crack was a hole into some other room—a place where green fires burned. Or maybe some kind of creature lived inside the crack, slowly widening it day by day!

Just as he thought this, something appeared at the edge of the broken plaster. Eugene's mouth turned dry as dust as he watched a small black snaky thing squirm out of the crack and touch the edge of his hamster cage. Terrified, Eugene screamed for his parents.

The minute he opened his mouth the tendril whipped back into the crack. And even as his parents stumbled down the hall, the glow died away. By the time they switched the light on in his room, the crack was as innocent-looking as it had ever been.

"I saw something crawl out of the crack!" he sobbed as he pointed to the corner.

His dad crossed over to the wall and peered up at the crack. "What was it?" he asked, tilting his head to one side.

"I don't know," Eugene said, catching his breath. "But it was scary."

"It's all right, honey," his mother said, bending down to hug him.

"What's going on?" asked his sister. She stood in the doorway, rubbing her eyes.

"Eugene thought he saw something come out of the crack up there," his mom said.

"I don't see anything," his dad said, peering up at the shadowy corner.

"Maybe it was some kind of bug," Cindy offered.

"Could be," his dad agreed and left the room.

"I don't think it was a bug, Mom," Eugene ventured.

"What do you think it was?" she asked.

"I don't know. Some kind of monster."

"But, honey," she said, "that crack's been there for ages! Are you sure you weren't dreaming?"

Eugene nodded. Just then his dad came back in with a can of insect killer. He sprayed the sweet-smelling stuff straight into the crack.

"Ugh!" said his sister, holding a hand to her nose. "I'm getting out of here!"

"That should do the trick," he said, moving the cage farther away from the crack. He turned to smile at Eugene. "Okay?"

Eugene bit his lip and nodded. "Yeah. Thanks, Dad. Thanks, Mom."

His mom opened the window for some fresh air, then left the room with his dad. Eugene lay very still for a while. Then, feeling somewhat embarrassed, he switched on his small bedside light and closed his eyes to go to sleep.

He woke up the next morning and wanted to laugh. It had worked! With the light on, the monster from the crack wasn't able to enter his room. He sat up and happily turned off the light. He looked up at the crack in triumph.

Suddenly, his heart gave a loud thump before it fell into his stomach. He fought the urge to throw up while fear raced across his shoulders and back.

The hamster cage was empty! Eugene vividly remembered his pet being there the night before, when his dad had moved the cage away from the bug spray.

He climbed to his shaky feet and stood on the bed. Yes, it was gone. Not just laying down or hiding under the straw. His knees buckled, and he fell to the mattress. After a moment he got up, dressed quickly, and ran downstairs.

Cindy was sitting at the table. Their mother was standing at the sink.

"Did either of you see my hamster?" Eugene demanded.

"Huh?" Cindy stared at him blankly.

"My hamster is gone. Did you take it?"

Cindy shook her head. His mom also denied having seen or touched the missing pet. Eugene felt something cold wrap itself around his heart.

"Why?" his mother asked.

"Because it was there last night, and now it's missing!" He raced back to his room, followed by his mother and sister. His mother stood next to the bookcase and looked into the cage.

"He must have gotten out somehow," Cindy said.

"How?" Eugene demanded. "He can't climb walls, you idiot!"

"Eugene," his mother warned. "Take it easy. He's not here, so he must have escaped somehow. Don't worry, he'll turn up."

Eugene took a deep breath. "Could you fix that crack today?" he asked his mom.

"Of course," she agreed, stepping away from the shelf. "Don't worry about it."

When Eugene got home that day, his mom took him to his room right away. The crack was covered with a bright white layer of fresh plaster.

Eugene suddenly felt a lot better. He smiled and threw himself at his mom to hug her.

She laughed. "That old crack was pretty deep. But I kept shoving plaster in there until it was filled up, then I smoothed it over."

"Thanks, Mom," Eugene said with all his heart.

He almost looked forward to sleeping in his own room that night. After wishing his parents good night, he stared for a long time at the corner. Nothing happened. He smiled, rolled over on his side, and quickly fell asleep.

He never knew what woke him up. Was it the steady, insistent tapping? Or the small sound of plaster falling to hit a wooden shelf? Or the gritty, slithery sound of something poking its way through a plaster-covered hole?

Eugene was lying on his back, and he only had to shift his eyes to see the source of the sounds. A pencil-thin beam of green light shot out through the hole in the new plaster. The black worm thrust its tip out and around the hole, like a tongue licking the lips of a thirsty animal.

Eugene knew he had only one chance. Barely breathing, he reached over and felt for the lamp. His fingers found the switch, and in a moment bright light filled the room. But the monster stayed! If anything, it seemed to work more frantically at the plaster. Eugene saw another piece fall to the shelf. The tentacle moved in the air as if waving at him. He felt like screaming.

But he didn't. Instead he ever so slowly slid open his nightstand drawer. Never taking his eyes off the crack, he found his scout knife and pried open the blade. Then he placed his feet on the floor and crept over to the corner.

The tentacle froze in place. Before he knew what he was doing, Eugene jumped on the bottom shelf and boosted himself up to slice deeply into the thing.

It whipped back into the opening, then shot out with such force that the remaining plaster showered down on Eugene. He jerked back, and the shelf collapsed under him. With a crash, the entire set of books, the cage, his models and everything else landed on the floor with him.

In a moment his parents arrived, followed closely by his sister. His dad took in the collapsed shelves, the chipped-away plaster, and Eugene's knife.

"Eugene!" he shouted. "What on earth are you doing?"

Eugene could tell his dad was pretty mad. "It came back," he stammered, "and I . . . I tried—"

"Spare me," his dad said, holding up his hand. Then he took a deep breath. "All right." He looked around. "Okay. Cindy, Eugene is going to sleep in your room for tonight and you'll sleep in here. We'll work this out in the morning."

"What?!" she shrieked. "Dad, that's not fair!"

Their father just looked at her. "Will you please help me out with this?"

Eugene wanted to disappear. And he could see from the look in Cindy's eyes that he would probably never live this down. She nodded.

"Thank you," his dad said. "Now, let's all get back to bed." Cindy darted a killing look at Eugene as she climbed into his bed. His father took him by the arm down to Cindy's room and didn't let go until he got there.

"I think I know what you're up to," his dad said in a surprisingly calm voice. "But we're not going to put you and Cindy back in one room together." He turned and left the room. Eugene's mom came in soon after and quietly kissed him good night.

After they were gone, Eugene's mind began working. It had all happened so fast. How could they think he had made it all up? Why would he do such a thing? His mind darted from one thought to the next. He lay back onto the pillow and fell asleep, still trying to figure out what to do.

In the morning, he woke with a start. Something tickled the back of his mind. Then he recognized his surroundings and remembered.

What if the monster had come back last night? It would have been pretty angry after he had stabbed it. He never should have let his sister stay in that room!

He jumped out of bed and ran down the hall. His mother was knocking gently at his sister's door to wake her up. Eugene's breath seemed to stick in his throat as she pushed the door open.

"All right, all right," his sister moaned from under the covers. "I'm up." Eugene stared openmouthed as his sister stretched and sat up.

"What are you staring at, jerk?" she asked when she saw him.

Eugene just shook his head. "Nothing." He slowly chose some clothes out of his dresser and went down the hall to the bathroom.

Sure enough, the breakfast table became a family meeting. But Eugene barely listened as his dad accused him of trying to stir up trouble in the hope of either sharing a room again or getting the larger room for himself. He talked about Cindy growing up and Eugene needing to do the same. He talked about how powerful an imagination could be, about poltergeists, about sleepwalking.

But Eugene's mind kept replaying what he had seen, and he just couldn't believe it had been his imagination. On the other hand, why would the monster from the crack in the wall ignore his sister? Could it have been a dream? But what about the plaster? He hadn't even gone near it—sleepwalking or not!

Eugene mustered a half-hearted defense, but his dad had already decided to put him back in the old television room. Eugene spent the rest of the day actually dreading the final school bell.

That night, he felt like a criminal sitting down to his last meal. His parents tried to cheer him up, but he was too depressed to react. He listlessly watched television for a while to try and delay the moment. All too soon he got the nod from his dad—it was time to go to bed, no buts about it.

Like a soldier preparing for battle, he arranged his defenses. He switched on the bedside lamp. He got out his pocketknife, opened it, and set it on his nightstand. Then he brought out the can of bug spray he had hidden under his bed earlier. After that he slowly sank down under the covers and focused his attention on the crack in the wall.

Eugene stared at the crack until his eyes began to feel itchy and puffy. He rubbed at them and told himself to stay awake. He shook his head to clear it. But his eyelids dropped lower and lower until they stuck.

They flew open when he heard the tapping. Reaching for his knife, he twisted his head toward the crack. His arm froze but his heart was racing. He gagged as his throat convulsed.

There was something sticking out of the crack. But the black worm was gone. In its place was a finger! It stretched out of the crack, tapping its way around the rough edges.

"No," Eugene whimpered. He forced his rubbery muscles to lift himself out of bed and stumble over to his bedroom door. While keeping his eyes on the writhing finger, he tugged at the door. His sweating hands slipped off the polished doorknob, but finally he got it open and thrust himself out. His sister was standing in the dark hallway, watching him.

"Cindy!" he gasped in a high-pitched wheeze. "It's there! I swear it!"

"We believe you," she said in an alien voice that stopped his every bodily function. His eyes were the only part of him that seemed to work as he watched two black, snaky tentacles shoot out of the sleeves of her nightshirt and wrap hungrily around his neck.

A Jarring Experience

---

nd this is a very good sample of a trilobite fossil," said Mr. Kegan, the science teacher. The class crowded around the display case. "Who remembers in which period these creatures existed?"

Gary wandered off to one side of the huge room while his classmates started shouting answers. The room was part of a whole floor in the museum dedicated to fossils and geological items from the Paleozoic era. Gary was interested, but only barely. What he really wanted to see was the Ancient Civilization section, with mummies and gold and weapons and cool stuff like that. But instead the class had spent most of the day in this section, and the museum would be closing soon.

Gary sat on a bench and stared gloomily

toward his classmates as they moved on to another display. He hadn't thought it was possible to be bored on a field trip to a museum, but Mr. Kegan somehow managed it. In fact, Gary almost wished they were back at school—at least class would be over by now!

"Hello," said a voice behind him. Gary turned to see a boy about his age. He had tanned skin and a mop of black hair hanging over his dark eyes.

"Hi," Gary answered, a little startled.

The other boy sat on the bench. "My name's Alexander, but you can call me Alex. Is that your class?"

"Huh?" Gary looked. "Oh, yeah. We're on a field trip." He turned to face the other boy. "My name's Gary."

"I hate field trips," declared Alex. "They always want you to look at all the boring stuff instead of spending time with the things you really want to see."

"Yeah," agreed Gary. "Like the mummy display."

"You like mummies?" Alex asked excitedly. "Oh, man, then you've got to see them here!"

Gary rolled his eyes. "Great. I wish you hadn't told me that." He sighed. "I think we have to leave soon."

Alex nodded in sympathy.

"How about you?" Gary asked after a moment. "Are you here with your school?"

Alex shook his head. "No, I came with my dad, but he dropped me off so I can pretty much do what I want."

"Must be nice," Gary said.

"Hey," said Alex. "Why don't you stay with me? Then after the museum closes I can have my dad take you home."

Gary was tempted. His own parents were out of town for another three days, and he and his sisters were staying with his cousins. With eight other kids in the house, Aunt Rita probably wouldn't notice if he were home or not.

"My teacher would never allow it," he pointed out.

"Really?" asked Alex. He thought for a moment. "I have a plan. Stay right here and don't move. I'll be right back."

Gary watched Alex dart off through a doorway. He felt excited at the thought of something interesting saving this day from total ruin. He studied the rest of the class to see if anyone was watching him.

Suddenly a fire alarm blared through the quiet halls. Gary jumped up as his classmates began screaming and running in every direction. Mr. Kegan was shouting orders, but nobody could hear him. Museum security guards began quickly herding people out of the room. Gary took a step toward the exit when Alex appeared in front of him.

"Come on!" he shouted over the loud noise. "Follow me!"

"What about the alarm?" Gary asked.

Alex grinned devilishly. "It's false! I set it off! Now come on, before they kick us out!"

They ducked through a doorway back into a room full of mineral and gem exhibits. Gary could hardly believe what he was doing as he followed Alex—sneaking along the walls and ducking behind display cases whenever an adult ran by. But it was so exciting that he couldn't stop himself.

"This is crazy!" Gary whispered at one point.

"Yep," agreed Alex. "But we'll have the museum all to ourselves!"

Soon the museum was empty. The two boys stopped for a rest under the enormous bones of an Allosaurus.

"There'll be fire fighters checking the place out," Gary panted. "And Mr. Kegan's sure to tell them that I'm missing."

"No problem," Alex assured him. "As long as they don't see us, you can tell your teacher that you ran outside and got a ride home."

"But what if we're caught? Then we'll get blamed for setting off the alarm!"

Alex shook his head. "No way. We're just two frightened kids who got lost in the confusion."

Gary pondered this. It might actually work. He felt like laughing. This was without a doubt the most incredible thing he'd ever done!

After a few minutes they crept out of their hiding place and snuck through the deserted halls. Every now and then they could hear people shout to one another and the echo of footsteps. They reached a staircase and had to duck behind a marble statue as a figure dressed in a yellow fire fighter's suit came down.

"Did you know the Ancient Civilizations floor is supposed to be haunted?" Alex whispered while they waited for the fire fighter to pass.

"What?" Gary asked. "Really?"

Alex shrugged. "Supposed to be."

"By what?"

"Nobody knows. But they say that late at night strange noises come from the Egyptian room. And one morning a guard was missing. All they ever found was his hat—right by the mummy display where we're going!"

"Where did you hear about this?"

"One of the guards told me earlier."

Gary smirked. This sounded like a lot of bad movies he'd seen. "You mean like some kind of mummy's curse?" he asked skeptically.

Alex nodded. "Yeah! That's what he said."

"I don't believe it," Gary said definitively.

"How come?"

Gary snorted. "Mummies are just the preserved bodies of people who died a long time ago."

"But what if the embalming process was so good that the body didn't realize it was dead?" Alex asked. "Or what if the spirit was trapped and, when the tomb was opened, it got sucked back into the body?"

Gary laughed. "No way! The body's useless! First the organs were taken out of it through a hole cut in the back. Then the brain was sucked out through the nose!"

Alex winced. "Gross."

"Yeah," continued Gary, warming to his subject. "Then the organs were put into these big jugs called canopic jars. And finally the body was dried out and wrapped in cloth soaked with all kinds of oils and stuff."

Alex laughed. "All right! I give up. Let's go check them out."

They cautiously made their way across the open space to the stairs. Alex took them two at a time, but Gary was more careful.

At the top of the stairs was a large room with glass cases protecting gold jewelry and ancient pottery. The walls were painted with hieroglyphics. Although the sunlight was fading from the high windows, Gary couldn't see Alex anywhere.

"Alex," he whispered. There was no answer. Gary smiled and made his way further into the room full of Egyptian artifacts. He could see the hulking stone sarcophaguses against the wall to his right, and he threaded his way over to them.

"Alex," he hissed. Suddenly, something grabbed him by the neck. Gary jumped and yelled.

"All right, kid. Calm down."

Gary turned around to face a fireman. The man was smiling as if he had enjoyed scaring Gary.

"What are you doing here?" the fireman demanded. "The museum's supposed to be empty."

Gary tried to control his pounding heart. "I was here with my class, but I got lost when the alarm went off."

The guard gave a bark of laughter. "Nice try, kid." He started pulling Gary to the security phone on the wall next to a sarcophagus.

"Wait," Gary said. "I really did get lost. I was looking for my friend. We came with his dad."

The fireman stopped and turned to face him. "Look, kid. I don't care if you were here with the director of the museum! My orders are to get this place cleared for reopening. And until that's done, nobody gets in here!"

Gary was just beginning to realize that he might be in trouble when something stopped his mind from thinking at all.

The sarcophagus behind the fireman slowly swung open. Inside was a dried-up brown thing that looked less like a movie mummy and more like a shriveled piece of meat. It had been wrapped so long that the bandages themselves had become part of the creature.

Gary's eyes bulged as two brown, skinny arms struck out and wrapped their hands around the fireman's throat. The man tried to fight, but before he could do anything Gary heard a wet crunch, and the fireman's throat disappeared in a spray of blood.

Then, with terrible speed, the thing pulled the man into the coffin and the lid slammed shut.

Gary stood there for a moment, then fell to his knees and vomited.

"Wow, what a mess!"

Gary swung his head up in shock. "Alex!" he nearly screamed. "You won't believe . . . I mean I don't . . . we gotta get out of here!" Gary was hysterical and knew it.

"Yeah," said Alex, stepping closer. "Those new mummies are pretty gruesome."

Gary's mouth hung open as he tried to wrap his thoughts around what Alex was saying. He watched blankly as Alex opened a small, child-size sarcophagus.

"New ones?" Gary stammered.

"Yeah, the ones that have just woken." Alex patted the closed lid of the fireman's tomb.

"You know a lot about mummies," Alex continued in a horribly casual tone. "Did you also know that magic formulas were placed with the dead of the most powerful families? They were called coffin texts." .

Alex stepped over to Gary and with no effort lifted his fear-frozen body to its feet. He then placed Gary into the small sarcophagus. Realization began to dawn in Gary's eyes, and his brain sent frantic messages to his legs to run. But it was too late.

"Some coffin texts describe how the dead body can come back to life by replacing the organs stored in its canopic jar with fresh ones," Alex said conversationally as he placed a hand on Gary's chest and began to dig his fingers into the flesh.

"Of course," he said with a strong push forward that tore skin and bones, "the problem then becomes making sure I always have fresh organs in the jar."

The Write Stuff

hat'cha working on now?" Molly asked her Uncle Steve from the side of his desk.

"Same old stuff," he said without turning away from the computer screen.

"More horror stories?"

He put his elbows on the desk and took off his glasses while he rubbed his eyes. "Yep," he answered. "Trying to come up with new and exciting ways to scare you kids to death."

Molly laughed. "Great! Need any help?"

He smiled and put his glasses back on. "No thanks. I think I've stolen enough of your ideas for now. Besides, I'm feeling pretty good tonight—I think it's going to be a good night." He ruffled her hair. "Thanks anyway."

"Sure." She hugged him briefly. "Good night."

Molly padded to her room where her Aunt Joyce tucked her into bed. As she waited for sleep to come, she listened to her uncle tap away at the computer in his study. Aunt Joyce was her mom's sister, and Molly had come to stay with them for three weeks while her parents went to Europe for a vacation. Although her aunt and uncle didn't have any kids of their own, Molly was having a good time staying with them. Uncle Steve was really funny, and was always telling jokes or quirky stories. Aunt Joyce was always ready to play a game with Molly when she wanted to.

Molly turned over on her side. Usually she fell asleep right away, but her uncle's typing was really bothering her tonight for some reason. With a sigh, she closed her eyes and refused to open them.

She woke in the middle of the night. She held her breath, but if it had been a noise that had woken her, it did not repeat itself. She glanced over at her bedside clock, but its display was blank.

She frowned. Was that what had woken her? Had something caused the power to go out? She threw back her covers and tiptoed softly to the door of her aunt and uncle's room.

"Aunt Joyce," she whispered as she pushed open the door.

There was no reply. Molly stepped into the room. "Uncle Steve?"

Faint moonlight spilled through the window and washed over the big, empty bed. Molly stopped, stunned.

"Aunt Joyce? Uncle Steve?" She ran a hand over the bed as if maybe the adults had been turned invisible. But they really weren't there! It looked as if the bed had never been slept in.

Molly shivered, feeling very small and defenseless. She twisted the knob of a bedside lamp, but there was still no power.

"Aunt Joyce?" she called, walking cautiously into the hall. Her voice seemed to fall flat in the still house. There was no answer. Molly shivered again and walked quickly down the hall to her uncle's study.

The study was also deserted. The chair where he had been sitting earlier was pushed against the desk. The desk itself was bare except for the dark computer.

"Uncle Steve?" This time Molly's voice came out as a sob. Where were they?

Then she heard a noise coming from the front of the house. Her hair felt disconnected from her head as her mind identified the noise. It was the creaking of the old floorboard in front of the fireplace.

Molly willed her legs to move. Maybe her aunt

and uncle were just out for a ride. Or maybe they're dead, the black part of her mind whispered.

Chewing her lower lip furiously, she crept out of the study and inched down the hall to the dining room. It was empty in the moonlight, and she slowly poked her head around the corner of the hall.

The living room was also empty. The couch and chair sat solidly in the middle of the room, and Molly could see there was nothing in front of the fireplace. The dark tank of the aquarium reflected a pale light. She thrust her head a little further into the room.

Suddenly the glass exploded as the aquarium disintegrated. Then rising over the metal stand was the immense body of a crab.

Molly gasped as she recognized the monster. It was the crab she had found on her field trip last week. She had never seen anything like it and had brought it home.

As if it had heard her, the crab took three clacking steps in her direction. Then two tendrils waved in front of its mouth and shot across the room, wrapping themselves around her body.

"No!" Molly screamed as the slimy, ropy arms pulled her closer. She could see the crab's mandibles opening in anticipation.

Then it suddenly disappeared, and Molly

fell to the floor on legs too weak and shaking to hold her. What was happening? She screamed for her aunt and uncle, tears welling up in her eyes.

"It must be a dream," she decided out loud. "I'm having some kind of nightmare. If I yell loud enough, I'll either wake myself up or someone will come."

She screamed again at the top of her lungs. The sound bounced off the walls, but nothing happened. Now the tears flowed freely down her cheeks.

"Oh, rats!" Molly's uncle said. He brutally erased the last few paragraphs he had been working on.

"What's the matter?" her aunt asked, looking up from her magazine.

"I don't know. I thought things were going to be easy tonight. I really felt, you know, powerful when I sat down. But nothing seems to be working."

"Like what?"

"Well," he said, turning around to face her. "I had this idea for a giant crab monster. Maybe the kid digs it up at a beach and brings it home."

"Sounds all right."

"Nah," he shook his head. "Too dumb. That

whole digging-up-a-monster idea is pretty old."
He sighed. "Besides, some kids would probably
laugh at the idea of giant crabs—very B movie."
He turned back to the computer.

"I suppose you could always ask Molly for
some more ideas," she suggested with a giggle.

"Oh, sure," he answered without turning
around. "Very funny. Maybe we should ask your
sister to let Molly stay with us whenever I've got
a deadline to meet!"

Joyce laughed and turned back to her
magazine.

———

Molly stopped crying after a few minutes. She
didn't know what had happened to her, but she
mustered her courage and got to her feet.

She went back to her bedroom and flipped the
light switch. There was still no power.

"Oh!" she growled. She went to her closet to
get dressed, but froze as she stared at the empty
shelves and clothes rods. A tingling suspicion
rippled the hairs on the back of her neck.

Running into her aunt and uncle's room, she
slid open the closet door. It was empty, too!
Then she ran into the kitchen and began pulling
out drawers—all empty. Sobbing "no" over
and over again, Molly ran from room to room,

yanking open drawers and closets. The entire house was deserted, empty except for her and the furniture.

Then a fresh horror skipped down Molly's back. She moved like a sleepwalker to the front door and slowly opened it. There was nothing! No porch, no yard, no street, no other houses— the entire house was surrounded by a soft, white glow she had mistaken for moonlight.

Molly slammed the front door and ran to the back. Fumbling at the lock, she finally flung the door open.

The backyard was hazy, but at least it was there. Molly stepped out onto the patio that circled the pool. Barely able to see a thing, she stared into the mist that seemed to crowd right up against the walls of the yard.

Suddenly, the surface of the pool splashed upward like a volcano had erupted at the bottom. Molly watched in numb wonder as a green and brown tentacle shot out of the water. It swayed in the air for a moment, then dove toward Molly.

———⬧———

"Argh!" Uncle Steve yelled.

"Now what?" Aunt Joyce asked.

He sighed. "Didn't you tell me once that

you used to be afraid of a monster in the pool drain?"

"Yes. Is that what you're writing about?"

"Was writing about. It's just too obvious—the minute the kid gets near a pool you know he'll get sucked in by the drain monster. And how does it get there? Is it in all drains? Does it just go after kids?" He began erasing the text on the computer.

"I didn't know that monsters had to make so much sense," she said, trying unsuccessfully to hold in her laughter.

He held up his hand. "Try to contain yourself. I think I've got it."

⋙◆⋘

Molly pried her eyelids open after a moment. The pool was calm and empty. There was no trace of the thing that had been attacking her. She turned and ran back into the house.

Trying to think of what to do, her thoughts buzzed in her head like a swarm of angry bees. She couldn't make sense of her world. "Aunt Joyce?" she cried forlornly as she wandered through the empty rooms. "Uncle Steve?"

She found herself back in the living room. The aquarium was now whole, and there was no trace of the crab monster. "Of course," Molly said angrily. Then she laughed wildly, feeling out of control.

She threw herself down on the sofa and stared blankly ahead of her. She felt as if she should be doing something, but was not at all sure what.

Slowly, a black shape oozed out of the fireplace like a monster awakening. Molly stared blankly as the thing billowed out over the hearth and flowed toward her. It looked and moved like it was made totally of smoke. Its wispy tentacles waved and coiled in the air. Its eyes reminded her of glowing embers.

Molly continued to stare at the creature, waiting for it to disappear like all the rest of the nightmares.

———◆———

"Got it!" her uncle Steve announced happily.

"Finally," said her aunt Joyce. "What did you decide on?"

He spun around in his chair. "A smoke monster! It's great! It lives in the chimney, so the house isn't safe. It can easily travel around, and its victims appear to have mysteriously suffocated."

Her aunt Joyce shook her head as her husband swung back and excitedly typed out his latest creation. "Your mind works in a very strange way," she said. "It's probably a good thing we don't have any children."

——◆——

The young girl tried to get up, to run away from the billowing smoke that seemed to have taken on a life of its own. She opened her mouth to scream, but the smoke gushed into her throat, choking her. She struggled madly but her oxygen-deprived muscles slowly grew still. The monster drifted away from her lifeless body, searching for its next victim.

A Family Outing

o you think there are going to be any bears?" Lynn asked her brother Nicholas.

"Nah," he answered. "It's too early in the season. They're probably still hibernating."

"Nicholas is right," agreed their mother from the front seat. "But even if there are bears around, they prefer to stay away from humans."

"I don't know. If they've just finished hibernating, a tasty little kid might look good," said their father, making a slurping sound. Their mother slapped him playfully.

Nicholas watched the scenery as they passed by pine trees and green meadows. It was officially spring and the hiking trails had been open for two weeks. Still, patches of snow lay in the shadows, and even though it was early morning, the sky was overcast and gray.

As the road burrowed into the heart of the mountain, the car climbed higher and higher. Eventually, they were driving on a dirt track that ended at a wide clearing.

Nicholas and Lynn jumped out of the back and their parents stood and stretched.

"Smell it!" their dad said, throwing his arms wide. "Fresh air! I love the mountains!"

Their mom took a deep breath and nodded in agreement. "You can still smell the snow."

Nicholas sniffed, but he couldn't smell anything. Then a snowball smacked into the side of his head.

Lynn was laughing and frantically digging into the snow for another missile. Nicholas ran over to a white patch and started scooping snow into a ball. Within seconds, snow was flying every-where. Even their parents took a few tosses.

"All right," their dad stopped them. "We've got to hit the trail."

He opened the back of the car and started unloading the backpacks. After everyone had changed into their hiking boots and shouldered their packs, they started off.

"How far are we going, Dad?" Nicholas asked after they'd been hiking a while. "Should we check the map?" He hoped his dad would stop to explain, giving them a chance to rest.

"Beryl Lake," his dad answered over his shoulder without stopping.

"Nice try," Lynn whispered from behind.

Nicholas sighed and continued walking. It seemed to him that they had been hiking all day, but when they stopped by the side of a stream for lunch, it was only a little past noon.

"There's still a lot of snow," Lynn noted as they sipped the icy cold water.

"We needed it," her father said, munching on a sandwich. "Especially after such a long drought." He looked around at the deserted mountain. "Besides, this way we can have the mountain all to ourselves!"

After a while they gathered their things and started hiking again. As they climbed higher, they began to see bigger snowbanks gleaming beside the trail, and soon their feet were crunching patches of snow on the trail itself.

When they finally reached the lake where they were to camp, Nicholas yelled with joy. The entire lake was surrounded by a white blanket! Pine trees ringed the lake, and the shade of their branches had kept what little sun there might have been from melting the snow.

They had to walk practically all the way around the lake until they could find a patch of rocky soil that was not under the trees and was also flat enough to pitch their tents. Then they spent the few remaining hours of late afternoon setting up camp and gathering firewood.

After dinner they sat around the fire for a while, until Lynn and Nicholas were sent to the tent they were sharing.

As they lay in their sleeping bags, Nicholas tried to scare his sister with tales of horrible monsters roaming the wild forests. But Lynn fell asleep almost immediately, and he had to lay awake by himself, listening to the night.

"I hope a bear eats her," he grumbled to himself after a weird noise made him jump.

When Nicholas woke up the next morning, his sister was gone. Moving like a giant snake, he bellied his way over to the front of the tent and pulled the flap aside.

The world had disappeared into a solid wall of fog. "Mom?" he ventured. His voice seemed to stick in the air in front of his face. "Dad?"

There was no answer, and he drew his sleeping bag a bit tighter around his shoulders. "Lynn?" he called, louder.

Suddenly a hand appeared out of the fog and wrapped around his neck. He screamed hoarsely and jerked himself backward into the tent, kicking wildly to free himself from the sleeping bag.

Lynn stuck her head into the tent, laughing.

"Hah! That's for all your gross stories last night!"

Nicholas lay back and let his heart stop pounding. Then he began kicking his way out of his bag again. "I'm going to get you!"

Lynn backed out, and he heard her laughing. He pulled on his pants and boots and crawled outside.

The fog swirled around him like white cotton candy. It was so dense that he could hear his sister—and knew she was close—but couldn't see her.

"All right, Lynn," he gave up. "Where're Mom and Dad?"

His sister appeared beside him. "Down by the water, arguing. Mom thinks it's silly to spend a week up here if the weather's going to be this bad. Dad's trying to convince her it'll get better."

Nicholas peered around blindly. "I don't know. I think I agree with Mom."

Lynn nodded. "Me, too. But poor Dad—he's been planning this for months."

In the end their mother prevailed. While Nicholas' dad cooked freeze-dried eggs over the portable stove the rest of them packed. After a quick breakfast they began picking their way back down the mountain.

But the fog only seemed to get worse as they descended. The narrow trail forced them to walk single file with their dad first, then Lynn and Nicholas, and their mom bringing up the rear. Nicholas found that he had to pay really close attention to the trail to make sure he didn't trip.

After a while they took a rest. The air was moist and cold, and everyone's breath floated around their heads like tiny clouds.

"It's freezing out here," Nicholas complained.

"That's why I put on my long johns before we left," Lynn said smugly.

Nicholas glared at her, then turned to his dad. "Can you guys wait a minute while I put mine on?"

His dad sighed. "All right. But hurry."

Nicholas threw his pack down and dug through to his thermal underwear. Then he went off the trail a little ways to strip down.

He was pulling his pants back on when he suddenly felt as if something were watching him. He whirled around, trying to pierce the fog with his eyes. The forest was still and quiet. He hurried into his boots and stumbled back down to his pack.

"About time, Wormy," Lynn greeted him as he stood there feeling foolish.

His dad levered himself off the rock he was sitting on. "Ready?"

They hoisted their packs and started hiking again. Nicholas' mother went up front to talk to his dad, and Nicholas lagged behind his sister. He could still barely see his own feet, and had to put his head down and follow his sister's footsteps.

After a few minutes, he realized that in his rush he had forgotten to lace his boots. He looked up to call to his sister, but changed his mind. He crouched down on a rock and quickly laced them.

When he stood back up, his family had disappeared! He took a few running steps forward, but stopped when he felt his ankle turn dangerously on a rock. "Hey, Lynn," he called. "Wait up!"

"Come on, Wormy," he heard her call from what seemed like a few yards in front. He started forward more carefully, and after a few moments he saw her vaguely through the fog. As soon as he saw her, she began walking again.

"Oh, thanks for waiting," he muttered to himself. "Jerk."

The trail continued, and Nicholas was unable to find any of yesterday's landmarks in the fog that still lay on the mountain. In fact, the fog made the trail seem more uneven and treacherous than it had been just the day before. He began to fantasize that he was walking in a cloud. Soon, he imagined, he'd come across a cloud city filled with all sorts of weird creatures!

"Come on," Lynn called, and he realized he had stopped in the middle of the trail. He hurried to catch up to her, but she remained a dark outline against the fog.

"Lynn," he called. "What's the hurry?"

She didn't answer at first. Then she stopped

walking. Nicholas puffed his way up to where she stood, unbuckling his waist belt and slipping his shoulders free of his shoulder straps. As he drew closer, something about the way she was standing struck him as odd.

"I wanted to make sure we were far enough away," she said.

"What?" he asked as he closed the last few feet between them. Then suddenly the freezing air enveloped his heart. He stopped.

The thing standing in front of him was not his sister. It was about the same height, but it was covered with dirty, yellowish fur. Its face was humanlike but with cat eyes and long, needle-like teeth.

"You see, Wormy," it said in a horribly perfect imitation of his sister's voice, "screams carry farther than you think in this weather. And I wouldn't want your family to be warned."

With one fluid motion Nicholas slid the pack from his shoulders, turned, and ran back the way he had come. The creature must have led him off on a different path. But he couldn't be that far from his family if that thing had been afraid they would hear him! The creature howled close behind, and his flesh crawled as he realized it was still using his sister's voice.

Relying on luck to keep him from falling, Nicholas sprinted down the trail. He knew he had never run this fast before. But he had to find his parents! And where was Lynn?

He heard rocks clatter behind him as the thing chased him. Don't look! his mind screamed. Concentrate on the trail! Now he could hear panting behind him as the thing drew closer.

Then he saw faint figures on the trail below him. "Mom!" he screamed. "Dad!" He pounded down the trail.

"Nicholas?" he heard his dad ask in surprise.

Nicholas sobbed for joy. The noises behind him had stopped as he got closer to his family.

But then his legs seemed to turn to rubber, and he skidded to a stop. Three more of the creatures were hunched over the bodies of his family! One crouched over his dad with one claw thrust into a steaming hole in his dad's back. It was this one that grinned horribly. "Nicholas," it repeated in his father's voice. "Bears aren't the only things that hibernate."

Nicholas fell to his knees, powerless to do anything as a cool, bony claw wrapped around his neck from behind.

Photo Finish

A my gasped and jerked her head up as a gust of rain clattered against the roof of her grandpa's attic. When she realized what it was she laughed nervously, half-expecting the rain to burst through the old shingles.

Amy's grandpa had been sick for a long time, and although she didn't know exactly what was wrong with him, she had finally gotten used to the idea that he wasn't going to recover. It hadn't really been a surprise when Amy's parents had gently told her that they were taking him to a hospice—a place where he could have constant supervision as he daily drew closer toward the grave.

After they visited the hospice, Amy and her parents drove to her grandpa's house to start packing things for storage. It had been raining all that weekend, and Amy's mood was as dreary as the weather. While her parents rummaged around downstairs, Amy went up to the attic.

She poked through old trunks filled with clothes and dusty books, ancient toys and yellow magazines. She wasn't even trying to pack, but simply wanted to keep her mind off her grandpa. Then she noticed something under the sagging brass bed, and she reached for it and pulled it out.

It was an old brown paper bag with a camera inside—the kind that spat the photo out right after it was taken. Although it looked worn, it didn't seem to be broken. Amy checked the bag to see if there was anything else interesting and found some snapshots of people.

"They must've been Grandma and Grandpa's friends," she murmured. There was even a photo of her grandfather, taken when he was still healthy enough to smile and laugh.

Amy placed the camera back into the bag and went downstairs.

"Mom," she said when she found her mother in the kitchen. "Look what I found!" Amy pulled the camera out of the bag and held it up.

Her mother turned around and smiled. "Where did you find that?"

"Upstairs in the attic. It was under the bed with some old photos."

"The brass bed?" Her mother came over and looked into the bag. "Oh look! There's your grandfather." She leafed through the other photos but didn't recognize anybody.

"Can I keep it, Mom?" Amy asked after her mother had handed back the pictures.

"I don't see why not. We'll ask your dad to stop and buy some film on our way home. Then you can see if it works."

After spending the rest of the afternoon sorting through her grandfather's things, Amy and her parents headed for home. Her dad stopped at a drugstore and bought some film, which Amy loaded carefully. Then she pointed the camera at herself and pressed the button. After a satisfying whirring sound, the camera shot out a snapshot.

Amy studied the blank surface anxiously. In a moment a ghostly image began to appear. Slowly it solidified until her own picture appeared.

"Hooray!" she shouted. "It works!"

The next day Amy took her new camera to school. She spent the day taking photos of her friends and classmates. She got Jana, her best friend, and three other friends together for a group shot. Then she took snapshots of her teachers and the school grounds.

By the end of the day she had used up the whole roll of film. All the pictures had turned out clear and focused, but for some reason Amy felt secretly guilty about enjoying her poor grandpa's camera so much. The more she thought about it the more she felt sorry for him. In fact, by the time she got home she was so depressed that she put the camera and the photos in her desk drawer and forgot about them.

Not too long after that, Amy started to feel ill. She would wake up in the morning with pain in her neck or shoulders, her muscles so tight that they gave her headaches. Then she began to notice that her feet were always cold, and later her hands felt icy, too. Within a couple of days, both her hands and feet were numb.

Her muscle pains got steadily worse, until it seemed like she was always stiff. Finally, when she was barely able to get out of bed one morning, she said something to her parents.

"How long have you felt like this?" her mother asked in concern.

"I don't know, Mom. Maybe a week."

"It sounds like what your grandpa had," her dad said with a puzzled voice.

They took her to the doctor, but he couldn't find anything wrong. Test after test showed nothing, and Amy became stiffer and stiffer each day.

As her muscles knotted themselves into new

and immobile shapes, Amy began to lose control of her body as well. Soon all she could do was sit in her room, twisted into a bizarre shape. None of the doctors she had seen knew what was happening to her. They thought it might be some kind of new disease or a variation of an old one. But Amy finally realized what was happening when she overheard her parents talking one afternoon. They were trying not to let her see how scared they were, but they sometimes forgot that she could hear as well as she ever could—she just couldn't react to the news.

"I'm telling you," her father whispered angrily to her mother as they stood outside her door, "the school is at fault! They must have served some kind of contaminated food during lunch."

"But you heard what Mr. Vera said," her mother answered. "Not all of the children that have this thing ate in the cafeteria that day."

"Then it was in the water! Or something else! How could half the kids in that school have the same thing Amy has if it wasn't spread around by something at the school?"

Amy couldn't hear the rest of the conversation because her parents had moved away from her door. But she had heard enough to realize that she was not the only one suffering from this strange disease.

The next clue came a couple of days later, when her cousin Olive came over to see her. Amy's mind still worked, trapped as it was inside the helpless shell of her body. She could no longer control her limbs at all, and she could barely move even her mouth. She knew it wouldn't be long before even that stopped, and she would be locked into some distorted position for the rest of her life, unable to do anything but scream inside her head.

"Olive," she squeezed out. "Who else is sick?"

"You wouldn't believe it, Amy. It's real scary." Olive then went on to list nearly all of the kids in Amy's class. And nobody knew what was causing the illness.

Suddenly, Amy realized the horrible truth. All of the kids that were sick had been photographed by her the day she had taken the camera to school! As soon as she realized this, she knew with sickening confidence that it was true. In fact, she had actually been given the first clue weeks ago, when she had first begun having the same problems her grandpa had.

She spent the rest of the day devising a plan. She knew that it sounded incredible, so she wouldn't be able to tell anybody the awful truth. But she also knew that she didn't have much longer until her mouth stiffened into an eternal, drooling hole. When her mother came in, Amy